There's a BOOGEYMAN Under my Bed

BY:.Olga Fyne

Illustration by: Evelyn Worrell

ISBN: 978-1-7331472-0-0

Contact:

Phone: 516-880-5238

Facebook: https://www.facebook.com/amfyne

Twitter: https://twitter.com/amfyne

Poshmark.com/closet/fynemarketplace

LinkedIn: https://www.linkedin.com/in/dr-olga-m-fyne-471b4012/

Instagram: Olga Fyne

Dedication

This book is dedicated to my own grandchildren Matthias and Ethan and other children, who have experienced fear of some monstrous imaginative creature, at some point in their lives. I'm absolutely delighted that you have such creative imagination, but please always remember, that monsters and boogeymen are not real, they're only in your imagination.

“Mom!” called Anna.

“There’s a boogeyman under my bed!”

“Tell him to go away,” said her mother. “If I tell him to go away,” said Anna, “he might eat me when he comes from under my bed.”

"So, say it in a soft voice then," said Mom.

Anna told the boogeyman to go away in a soft voice, but she was still afraid.

She called again, “Mom!”

"Yes!" replied her mother.

"The boogeyman is still under my bed," said Anna.

"Tell him you love him," said her mother.

“What?” replied Anna. “Mom, are you crazy? If I tell him I love him, he will come into my bed.”

“Try it and see,” said her mother.

"I love you, boogeyman," said Anna.

She then called her mother again.

When her mother replied, Anna said, "Mom, I told the boogeyman I love him, but he did not answer."

“That’s because he’s happy,” said her mother.

Anna replied, “Now I’m not afraid anymore, Mother.”

Her mother replied, “Now give him a kiss and a hug and go to sleep.”

“Are you sure, Mom?” replied Anna.

“Of course I am dear,” replied her mother. “Boogeymen never hurt anyone.”

“Why, Mother?” asked Anna.

Mother replied, “Because boogeymen are only in your imagination.”

“Really?” asked Anna.

“Yes,” said mother. “It’s all in your head.”

“Mom!” called Anna again. “I am going to ask the boogeyman to sleep in my bed.”

"Go ahead," replied her mother.

Anna pretended to hug the boogeyman tightly, and soon she was in the land of dreams.

The next morning Anna and her mother talked about her experience with the boogeyman, and from that time on, she was no longer afraid of boogeymen. She told her friends at school about her experience and that boogeymen are only in their imagination.

When Mrs. Paddyfoot read the story: There's *a Nightmare in My Closet* to the class, Anna was able to make the connection to her experience with the boogeyman immediately and kept raising her hand. She could not wait to tell Mrs. Paddyfoot, that nightmares like the boogeyman are not real; they are only in the imagination.

About the Author

Dr. Olga Fyne is a Nationa*l Teacher Trainer* in Classroom Management, Differentiated Instruction and Literacy. She is a former teacher of the New York City Public schools for twenty-five years. Dr. Fyne works alongside her husband in pastoring the Beulah Church of the Nazarene in Brooklyn, NY.

She delights in sharing her original poems and rhymes with students, as she frequently visits schools and engages them in active listening, as they participate by singing, dancing and reciting those rhymes and poems.

Dr. Fyne is also an Educational Consultant. She is a gifted writer and author of several adult and children's books, which includes: My Shadow is a Copy-cat, My ABC Animal Book of Rhymes and Jingles and God is too big for your Hip Pocket. She preaches and teaches both nationally and internationally and resides with her husband in Woodmere, NY.

CONTACT THE AUTHOR

Phone: 516-880-5238

Facebook: https://www.facebook.com/amfyne

Twitter: https://twitter.com/amfyne

Poshmark.com/closet/fynemarketplace

LinkedIn: https://www.linkedin.com/in/dr-olga-m-fyne-471b4012/

Instagram: Olga Fyne